RAINTREE IS AN IMPRINT OF CAPSTONE GLOBAL LIBRARY LIMITED, A COMPANY INCORPORATED IN
ENGLAND AND WALES HAVING ITS REGISTERED OFFICE AT 264 BANBURY ROAD, OXFORD, OX2 7DY –
REGISTERED COMPANY NUMBER: 6695582

WWW.RAINTREE.CO.UK
MYORDERS@RAINTREE.CO.UK

DESIGNED BY HILARY WACHOLZ
ORIGINAL ILLUSTRATIONS © CAPSTONE GLOBAL LIBRARY LIMITED 2017
ILLUSTRATED BY NEIL EVANS
PRODUCTION BY KATHY MCCOLLEY
ORIGINATED BY CAPSTONE GLOBAL LIBRARY LIMITED
PRINTED AND BOUND IN CHINA

ISBN 978 1 4747 2909 3 (PAPERBACK)
20 19 18 17 16
10 9 8 7 6 5 4 3 2 1

BRITISH LIBRARY CATALOGUING IN PUBLICATION DATA
A FULL CATALOGUE RECORD FOR THIS BOOK IS AVAILABLE FROM THE BRITISH LIBRARY.

FADE TO BLACK

BY J. A. DARKE

TEXT BY ERIC STEVENS
ILLUSTRATED BY NEIL EVANS

raintree
a Capstone company — publishers for children

CONTENTS

CHAPTER 1

Mila Chun, fifteen years old, leaned her elbows on her desk and her chin on her fists. She was staring at him. Again.

"Mila," hissed the girl next to her.

Mila hardly noticed. Her eyes were on Ricky Chestnut, who sat at the front of the room. At the moment, their maths teacher Mr Hartly was lecturing about something-something-quadratic-something. Mila knew that if he caught her daydreaming one more time. . .

"Mila!" The hiss next to her became more urgent. Mila ignored it.

She wished she hadn't, because then came a pointy elbow in her side, and that got her attention.

Mila twisted and laid into her seat neighbour with a withering glare. She hissed back, "Ow! What is wrong with you?"

"What's wrong with *me*?" said Junie Weid, her neighbour, who also happened to be Mila's best friend and number-one antagonist. "You're the one about to be caught staring again."

Mila hadn't had a very close friend since Year 5 – four years ago now. That's when her best friend and next-door neighbour, April Oak, had moved away. Mila and April had always said they would keep in touch. But when middle school started, Mila never texted as often as she had meant to – or ever at all, really. Even when April had texted her, Mila just hadn't been good at staying in touch. Instead she had been focused on making new friends. Only she'd never made a friend as close as April. Sometimes she wished she had told April that, but . . . well, it had been so long now. Texting her out of the blue would just remind them both what a terrible friend Mila had been.

April's house had stayed empty for years, until the Weids moved in at the beginning of the summer before Year 9. Once school had started, and the girls realized they had almost all of their classes together, Junie had moved into most of the desks next to Mila, too.

Junie was nothing at all like April. Mila's old friend had been pretty and fun, always positive and sunny. Junie, though, was hot-tempered, and her searing glares were as often accompanied by a sneer as a shining smile. Still, the two girls had become fast friends. They'd spent most of the summer together. With school in full swing, they were now almost inseparable.

Even if Junie is at times a little . . . much. Mila chuckled to herself, thinking of her new friend.

"Mila. Sweetheart. Laugh if you want," Junie said. "But you're my friend, so please take some good advice."

"Oh, here we go," Mila said, rolling her eyes. In their short time together, she'd learned that Junie often believed she knew exactly what Mila should do in every situation. "Please, Junie. Won't you please school me in absolutely everything about life, oh wise one?"

"Make fun at your own peril," Junie said, leaning closer and risking the wrath of Mr Hartly. "I know of what I speak."

"About boys?" Mila said. It wasn't yet November, but Junie already had a collection of boys that seemed to hang on her every word. Sometimes they would even follow her around the school like rats after the Pied Piper, carrying her bags and books. A couple of them had even offered to do her homework – not that she needed any help. Junie was brilliant, in addition to being drop-dead gorgeous. In fact, Junie was so brilliant and gorgeous, Mila often found it irritating. Meanwhile, Mila wanted the attention of exactly one boy – Ricky – and she had no clue how to get it. "Yeah, I'll say you do."

"What is *that* supposed to mean?" Junie asked. She made a face like she was offended, but Mila knew her better than that. She was sure that Junie was thrilled to her French-manicured toenails to be called an expert on boys.

"Just say what you want to say," Mila said.

Mr Hartly glanced at them, so Mila put her pencil to paper, scribbled her name in the margin of her notebook, nibbled her rubber and then dotted the *i* with a smiley face. When she looked up again, he was back to ignoring her and Junie.

"Well, sweetheart," Junie whispered as she scribbled little drawings of puppies and kittens in her own notebook – she was actually pretty good at that, too – "I can promise you that Ricky will one hundred per cent go for you, and I can tell you just what to say to make it happen."

"Fine," Mila said. "So tell me."

But Junie didn't reply. Instead she pulled a book with a sky-blue cover out of her rucksack and passed it over to Mila. It was easily fifty computer-paper pages, bound together with big staples and thick black tape on one side. The cover said "The Real Mila" in big black type.

"What's this?" Mila said as she began thumbing the pages.

"Don't open it yet!" Junie whispered

urgently. "It's a script. I've been dying to give it to you."

"A *script*?" Mila said. "Are you kidding me? When did you do this?"

"Two weeks ago," Junie said with a half-shrug. "I've been . . . polishing it."

"Let me get this straight," Mila said. "You're so obsessed with me getting together with Ricky that you decided to go ahead and type up a script for me to follow? Without even checking with me first? What do you think my life is, a TV show? And why is this so huge?"

"All right, all right," Junie said. "If you don't want it, give it back." She reached for the book but Mila snatched it away.

"I didn't say that," Mila said. She shoved it into her rucksack. "I'll look at it later. Maybe there's something useful I can pull out of it."

The bell rang to end period five, and Junie

winked at her at just the same moment. Mila thought it looked almost like Junie had controlled the bell with the mere movement of her eyelid.

"I guarantee it," Junie said as she stood up and shouldered her rucksack. "*Very* useful."

* * *

"Ricky," Mila said. Her voice sounded hoarse. She cleared her throat and tried again. "Ricky," she said, this time louder. "I was wondering if you could help me with my maths homework." Then she felt silly. Was she really practising a play about her own life?

She sat on the brick wall on the side of the high school, which surrounded the flower garden outside the cafeteria windows. The most important aspect of this location was that it was out of sight of all the buses and kids waiting to be picked up.

With her parents always checking in on her,

her big brother at university texting all the time and Junie offering advice constantly, Mila always felt like she was on stage. Right now, she wanted privacy.

She cleared her throat and looked down at the book Junie had given her. "I was wondering if you could help me with my maths homework," she recited.

Mila coughed. She took a deep breath and a sip from her water bottle. It sounded so ridiculous – so scripted. She closed the book and tried it again, changing the wording slightly: "I am having *so* much trouble with the maths homework."

Ugh, she thought. *Try not sounding like an absolute moron, Mila!*

"Um, Ricky?" she tried once more, after another sip from her water bottle. Actually, this time it was more like a chug. "Did you understand the maths lesson today?"

Mila sighed and dropped her head forward,

knocking it against the water bottle that sat in her lap.

"Ow," she said, but she didn't pick her head up.

What was the point? She could practise all day, sitting there on the wall talking to herself. It was not going to work. Even using Junie's script for help, Mila had no clue how to talk to boys – especially boys like Ricky.

She could practise this stuff forever, but when it came time to delivering her lines – with Ricky's deep, soulful eyes looking down at her from under his flop of black hair – she would mess it up.

She always messed it up. Like the time she had tried to tell him that his shoe was untied and ended up tripping over him instead. Or the time she'd asked him how his cross-country meet went and then started coughing uncontrollably. There was no reason to think it would be different with the help of a script.

"Mila?"

She looked up, and there he was.

Because of course, Mila thought as she looked up into his rich brown eyes. *My life is becoming as predictable as a bad TV show.*

But worst of all, Ricky wasn't alone. He was flanked by four of his cross-country teammates, all wearing their red and gold vests and shorts.

After all, Mila thought sarcastically, *why would Ricky go anywhere without half of the school cross-country team?*

Mila heard laughter nearby. Giggling.

To Mila, it almost sounded like a laugh track from a TV show. She shook her head as if to shake the thought away. The laughter was still there. It made her face hot, and she turned red so easily.

"You okay, Mila?" Ricky said. "Are you feeling all right?"

"What?" Mila said. He had such a nice smile, and he was smiling at her.

"Your head was down," Ricky said. "You looked like maybe you were ill."

"Oh, yeah," Mila said, hyper aware of the script on her lap. She hoped Ricky wouldn't notice, but at the same time she desperately wanted to pore over it to find any way of salvaging this moment. "I, um, I'm fine. It's nothing. Thanks for asking."

"Come on, Chestnut," said one of Ricky's teammates, Henry something-or-other. He was a year older, and Mila didn't like him. His smile was not nice. It made his face squish up, and his braces seemed to always have food caught in them. Even so, he smiled all the time, but not in a friendly way. He smiled like a hyena that had stumbled upon a freshly dead baby antelope. This seemed fitting to Mila. Henry seemed to be teasing some quiet, younger kid or another every time she passed him in the hallway between her lunch hour and period five French class. "We have to catch the bus to the meet."

"You sure you're okay?" Ricky asked as he let his teammates drag him away. His mouth formed a crooked half smile, and a dimple popped on his right cheek. Mila thought it was the most adorable thing she had ever seen.

She nodded. She so wanted to flip through Junie's stupid script to see how to reply, but she couldn't look while he watched. Besides, her brain was busy taking mental photographs of Ricky.

"Okay," Ricky said. His smile dropped away as he got pulled farther along. "I gotta get going. We have a meet in Plainsville today. See ya, Mila."

He vanished around the side of the school, and it was all Mila could do to squeak out a tiny "Bye!" way too late.

Mila picked up her water bottle for another drink – empty.

"Might as well go home," she muttered to herself as she hopped down from the wall. She shoved Junie's script into her bag and started walking.

CHAPTER 2

Mila was about halfway home when she began to realize that the full bottle of water she had drunk so thoughtlessly while practising talking to Ricky had now resulted in a *very* full bladder. She started walking faster – fast enough that she zipped past three sixth-form girls who were walking in the same direction.

They giggled as she passed.

Rude, Mila thought. But she didn't stop to tell them off or explain herself. She didn't slow down in order to appear the tiniest bit cooler. She didn't even look at them.

Can't slow down, Mila thought. *The bladder matter is becoming urgent.*

From nearby, Mila heard laughter, but she didn't see anyone. They must have been inside a porch, or maybe inside near an open window, watching TV or just having a good time.

It almost seemed to Mila that the laughter had been in response to the little rhyme she had come up with in her mind – *the bladder matter.* She smiled to herself as she jogged on, almost home.

Mila rounded the corner onto Blueberry Road and sprinted to her house. The door wasn't locked. *Thanks for little miracles,* she thought as she burst inside, kicked her shoes off and hurried towards the bathroom.

"Whoa, whoa, whoa!" her mother said, getting up from the sofa. "Are you in too much of a hurry to say hello to your grandparents?"

Mila's smiling grandma and grandad rose from their seats. She hadn't even noticed them sitting in the living room in a couple of easy chairs across from her mother.

"Oh, hi," Mila said. She let her grandparents approach her for hugs. They moved very slowly.

The bladder matter, meanwhile, was getting more serious by the second.

"She's gotten so big," Grandad said, placing his hands on her shoulders. Mila thought maybe he'd shrunk since the last time she saw him.

"And so lovely!" Grandma said as she wrapped her arms around her granddaughter and pressed her lips to Mila's cheek.

Mila bounced and hopped. "It's really great to see you," she said, "but, um, *I really have to pee!*"

Mum gasped. Grandad nodded. Grandma looked a little shocked.

And from out of nowhere came uproarious laughter, men and women and children beside themselves with laughter. It sounded like it could have been right in the living room with them, but at the same time, it sounded miles and miles away, like the memory of a dream.

Mila spun around, trying to find the source of the hysterics, but all she could see was her living room, her mother, her grandma and grandad. And no one was laughing.

"Don't let us stop you!" Grandad said. "When you gotta go. . ."

There came more dreamlike laughter as Mila smiled, nodded and hurried to the little bathroom at the back of the house. She dropped her bag just outside the doorway, then slammed the door, her head spinning and her bladder near bursting.

When she left the bathroom just a couple

of minutes later, Mila was surprised to find the entire house dark.

Even stranger was the fact that there was absolutely no sign of Mila's mother or grandparents.

CHAPTER 3

"Hello?" Mila said as she moved slowly through the living room. She hit the light switch by the door to the kitchen, but nothing happened.

She hit it again. And then again. Only an eerie silvery blue light filtered through the sheer curtains in the front windows. Mila couldn't even see the street.

Power cut? she thought.

But wouldn't someone have said something? Wouldn't they have waited for her to come out, so they could all find their way around with a torch or candle? She had only been in the bathroom for a couple of minutes.

Mila hurried to the front window and pushed the flimsy curtain aside. The street lamps were out. She couldn't even see them, aside from the outline of the nearest lamp, black and slim at the foot of their driveway.

Wait a minute, Mila thought. *Why is it dark out? How late is it? I just got home from school.* She hurried towards the kitchen, her thoughts racing. *Oh my gosh, did I fall asleep on the toilet? I've heard about that happening to people. Did I miss dinner?*

She almost expected to hear laughter – like she had a few times already this weird afternoon – but there was nothing. It was quieter than quiet, and darker than dark. There was no hum from the refrigerator, not a whirr from the TV in standby mode.

Mila ran into the kitchen, and it was dark too. No green numerals on the oven's clock.

No light coming in through the big sliding glass door to the back garden.

"Where is everyone?" Mila shouted. "Did we lose power?"

Mila thought about checking the trip-switch, but that would mean finding her way down the pitch-black basement steps. Instead, she peered through the sliding door into the back garden with her hands cupped around her eyes. If it was dinnertime, and if Grandma and Grandad were over, maybe Dad would be barbecuing outside. The season was still warm enough for it.

But no. The back garden was an inky pool of total darkness. If Mila squinted, she could just make out the back of the garage, the edge of the deck and the outline of Dad's big barbecue. Or she thought she could. The more she stared, the darker and murkier the scene became, until there seemed to be nothing beyond the patio doors at all.

This wasn't just odd anymore. It was frightening, and panic rose in Mila's chest and fluttered there like an agitated moth. Just then, she remembered her phone, which was sitting in her bag outside the bathroom door. She hurried – as much as she could in the pitch dark – through the swinging door out of the kitchen to get it.

"There you are!" Mum said as Mila burst into the living room, which was suddenly bright and familiar and warm. Everything looked normal. Mum, Dad, Grandma and Grandad all stood by the front door. Grandad was helping Grandma put on her light jacket.

Mum grabbed her purse out of the front closet. "We're heading to dinner. Aren't you ready?"

"Ready?" Mila said. Her skin tingled, cold and then hot. She felt confused and relieved and frightened all at once. What time was it? Where had everyone been? "But – you were gone . . . everyone was gone. It was completely dark."

Dad checked his watch. "Let's get moving," he said as if he didn't hear her.

Mum dug around in her handbag. Grandma and Grandad shuffled through the open front door. They just ignored Mila, as if she hadn't said anything at all.

"Anthony is meeting us in ten minutes, and I don't want to be late," Dad added.

Someone cheered.

"Anthony is coming?" Mila said. She grabbed her bag and joined her family at the door to slip on her shoes. Mila's big brother had started at a little university five hours away this autumn. He hadn't had much time to come home. "I didn't even know he was visiting!"

"Oh, I'm sure I mentioned it," Mum said, urging Mila out of the door. As Mila passed her, Mum leaned in close and whispered in her ear, *"Please* stick to the script. You're throwing me off."

"What?" Mila said. "What script?" But Mum was gone, already halfway to the car in the driveway.

CHAPTER 4

Though they got along well enough, Mila and her brother Anthony didn't agree about everything. In fact, there were a lot of things they didn't agree about. Fashion, music, politics, film and TV – Mila and Anthony would never see eye to eye. The only thing they ever agreed on was food – particularly their favourite restaurant, Etta's Pizza Palace. It was the one they always picked for birthdays and celebrations.

"Best pizza in the world," Anthony said after they'd ordered. He rubbed his hands together in anticipation.

"Anthony," Mum said. "You've never *been* anywhere but here."

Mila thought about it. Surely Anthony had been to other restaurants. Surely *she'd* been to other restaurants. But she couldn't think of a single one aside from Etta's.

"And the university," Anthony pointed out. "I've been to university." He twisted his face in confusion. "There's no decent pizza down there, though."

The table erupted with laughter. To Mila it sounded like a crowd of people bursting into hysterics. Mila laughed at first – but when the laughter seemed to grow too loud, like hundreds more people had joined in, she cut off her laughter and scanned the room. But Mum and Dad seemed like they were barely chuckling, and Grandma only shook her head with mild disapproval. Grandad seemed to be nodding off.

Mila gently squeezed his arm. "Grandad?"

"Heh, what?" he sputtered, flinching in his chair. He sat up and blinked, staring around the restaurant in confusion. "Where am I?"

More laughter. Mila looked around – maybe other patrons in the restaurant were laughing at them. *Rude*, Mila thought, but no one was watching them, nor even smiling. Even odder, when she looked back at her own table, the food was already there. Mila was sure they had only ordered a few seconds ago.

"You dozed off," Mila's mum said to Grandad. "We're at dinner."

"Right," Dad said. "You were just about to get the bill."

More laughter. Mila spun, trying to find who was laughing, but she found only straight faces – strangers in couples and groups of four, speaking quietly. Actually, now that Mila thought of it, the strangers seemed to not be speaking at all. Their expressions bland, they seemed to be just moving their lips and pretending to talk. Maybe they had been laughing, and now they were trying to cover it up.

"Stop it, honey," Mila's mum said with a smirk. She gave Mila's father a gentle nudge with her elbow. "*We're* buying dinner, of course."

Mum grabbed the bill as the waiter dropped it at the table, and Mila's head was spinning. She hadn't eaten yet – she was sure of it. But her plate was gone, and Anthony was leaning back in his chair with his hands on his stomach and pizza sauce around his lips.

"That was excellent," he said. "As always."

Dad burped into his hand. Mila rolled her eyes as chuckles rolled through the restaurant.

"I'm stuffed," Dad said, patting his belly. "You've got some sauce on your lip, Mila."

"Impossible," Mila said as she grabbed her napkin. "I haven't even eaten y–". But she dabbed her lip, and sure enough, a spot of bright red tomato sauce appeared on the napkin.

"Mila, don't be silly," Mum said. "You did some damage on that pizza!"

Anthony chuckled, Dad nodded in agreement and Grandma giggled to herself. But laughter surrounded Mila, too loud to have come from just her family.

Mila, though, could've sworn she hadn't eaten a thing. But then again, she wasn't hungry, exactly, and there had been the tomato sauce on her lip.

I guess I must have eaten if everyone thinks so, Mila thought. It had been a long and unusual day. Mila's head swam with confusion, and soon she felt woozy.

"I think I must be coming down with some–" she started to say, but just then the waiter reached across the table for the bill. He knocked Mila's full glass of pop, spilling the whole sticky mess right onto her lap.

"I'm so sorry!" the waiter said.

The air echoed with laughter again, this time peppered with groans and disappointed gasps. The waiter took a hand towel out of his apron pocket and began to dab at Mila's thighs, where most of the pop had spilled.

Mila jumped up from the table and knocked at the waiter's hand, blocking his inappropriate attempts to clean up the mess. She couldn't believe he would be so bold.

"It's fine," she snapped at him.

It wasn't fine, of course. In fact Mila was furious. She hurried to the bathroom, keeping her head down but feeling the eyes of every customer and staff member in the restaurant upon her as she crossed the crowded restaurant. The laughter rang in her ears, and this time Mila was sure she was the butt of the joke.

It was hopeless. Her jeans were sticky and wet, and her shirt would probably stain. It was one of her favourite shirts and practically brand new. What a waste.

Mila left the bathroom with her arms crossed over her belly, doing her best to hide the huge brown cola stain on her white shirt. She expected to find every eye back on her as she walked shamefully back to her seat. She wondered briefly if the waiter had at least managed to clean up the pop from her chair and the table.

But that didn't bother Mila for long, because when she returned to the dining area, it was empty and dark. And Mila's family – not to mention every other customer and every employee – was gone. Even Mila's bag and the phone inside had vanished.

It was just like what had happened at home only an hour before. Maybe all the bathrooms in her life were cursed. If her life had been a TV show, this episode could be called "The Bladder Matter" or "The Bad-Luck Bathroom" or "The Weird Bathrooms".

Mila hurried to the exit, hoping to find her family still in the car park. Could she have been in the bathroom so long that the restaurant had closed, and the staff had kicked everyone out?

Mila flung open the door and took a step into the car park, but the wind was bitter and loud. It whipped her cheeks and sent her hair into a frenzy, and it howled in her ears. Squinting against the terrible, unnatural weather, Mila saw a spot of light here and there. But the lights must have been miles away, because she saw no cars in the car park and no Mum or Dad, no grandparents or Anthony.

"Mum!" she called into the wind, but her voice seemed to bounce back at her, muffled and dull. As she pushed against the gusts, the lights around her – flickering in and out of vision – paled and went out.

Above her rose a ghostly image – hundreds and hundreds of huge, hazy faces looking down on her. They didn't smile. They didn't laugh. They didn't speak. They simply watched her, and it gave her a chill so deep and cold that her ears rang. The wind screamed, and it sounded so much like a human that Mila imagined those faces had been wailing at her.

Shivering and scared, Mila hurried back inside. When the door closed behind her, the quiet and stillness was almost as creepy.

Mila stumbled through the dark restaurant, gripping the backs of chairs and the edges of tables. She stubbed her toes and banged her knees till she reached the table where she and her family had been seated.

She ran her hands over the table to see if anything was there, but it seemed to be clean, wiped down. Any evidence that her family had been there was completely gone.

"I know I wasn't in the bathroom *that* long," she said aloud to the empty restaurant.

As she approached the kitchen door, Mila smelled fresh-cut wood. She poked her head through the doorway and smelled it even more strongly. The kitchen was dark. There was not even a lone staff member left doing the last of the dishes or scrubbing down the prep table.

"It's happening again," Mila whispered to herself, shaking her head. She hoped she was wrong even though she was almost certain she was right. She had to whisper, because while she could hardly bear to hear her voice echo in the emptiness again, she had to hear something. Her own voice let her know that she, at least, existed. "Just like at home this afternoon."

Mila thought about earlier, when she'd found herself abandoned in her dark house, only to find her family again seconds later. Was it really hours ago that she got home from school? Was that even possible? To Mila, it felt like only moments. All she knew was that somehow she was alone at Etta's restaurant, and it was obviously long after nightfall.

At home, she had gone into the kitchen just for a minute. When she'd exited the kitchen, everything was back to normal – if a bit later in the day than she'd thought. Maybe that would work here, too, at the restaurant.

Mila slammed the door open and stood in the middle of the big restaurant kitchen. She planted her hands on the cold, stainless steel prep table. She took a deep breath and then another to try to calm the violent fluttering in her lungs and chest. She counted to ten. She looked at the kitchen door and hoped to spot a sliver of light at the cracks – any hint that things were back to normal in the dining room. But it was still dark.

She counted to thirty, and then to thirty again. The doorway stayed dark. She couldn't wait forever.

Mila closed her eyes, took another deep breath and pushed the kitchen door open. She half-believed it would work – that her parents would look up from the table, or Anthony would freeze with his huge glass of pop halfway to his lips, and say, "Mila! Did you have to use the bathroom *again*?"

But none of that happened.

The dining room was still dark, silent and full of an icy air that sent a chill up Mila's spine. Tears sprang to her eyes. Although she didn't want to cry, she was far too overwhelmed to stop it. Mila was alone in the dark restaurant with no way of getting home and no way of finding her parents.

Mila eyed the front door. Beyond it was a swirl of darkness, wind and those terrifying wispy faces. All that made the possibility of stepping outside seem frightening. But staying where she was had begun to seem far worse. She bit her lip and opened the door.

The wind tore at Mila's face. She raised her arms in defence against the gusts and to block her view of the horrible faces that seemed to float like smoke at the horizon.

She pushed on through the car park. The farther she walked, though, the deeper Mila moved into the roaring wind and blinding darkness. And soon it was difficult to walk at all. Mila knew the way home – it was a long walk, but she'd done it more than once. However, without landmarks, without even street signs, she wasn't sure how far she could get. She could just barely make out the edges of the pavement.

Still, she pushed on towards a light in the

distance – a light she thought must be a street lamp along the old High Street. But the light didn't seem to get any closer, no matter how hard she pushed against the wind. In fact, it seemed to move, to swing around one way or another. At times it seemed to vanish entirely, only to reappear behind her.

It left Mila spinning. She had only been out in the windy darkness for a few moments when she gasped once and fell to her knees.

CHAPTER 5

Bzzz! Bzzz! Bzzz!

Mila opened her eyes. She was home now. She was in her bed, and the red numerals of the clock on her desk said 7:15.

The door flew open, and Mum burst in. She was frantic as ever, and slapped the alarm clock to stop its buzzing. "Good morning, my little pumpkin!"

"Mum," Mila groaned, sitting up and stretching her arms and back. She yawned. "I've asked you not to call me that anymore. I'm not a baby, you know."

Suddenly it all came rushing back. The

strange dinner at Etta's, the terrifying wind outside and those faces! In fact, all the oddness of the previous day swam around her mind. It couldn't have been real.

"Mum, I had the weirdest dream," Mila said.

"Hm?" Mum said as she shuffled through the mess of papers on Mila's desk. "I hope your homework is here somewhere. And finished."

"Did we have dinner with Anthony last night?" Mila said. "At Etta's?"

Mum smirked at her and pressed the back of her hand against Mila's forehead. "Are you feeling all right, Pumpkin?"

"Mum!" Mila said, pushing her hand away. "I'm not a pumpkin! And I'm not sick. Please just answer me. Did we or not?"

Mum sighed. "As you well know," she said, returning to her homework search, "that was last Friday."

Last Friday? Mila thought. *A week ago?* "What day is it now?"

"It's *Friday*," Mum said. "Again." She sighed so long and loud it sounded like a giant balloon deflating. "Really, Mila. I'm in no mood for one of your practical jokes. Now get up, get dressed and get going." Mum stepped into the hall, and then stuck her head back into Mila's bedroom to add: "Pumpkin!"

"Ugh!" Mila grumbled as she pulled the duvet over her head, and laughter filled the air – the laughter of hundreds of strangers, hooting and clapping and whistling. It echoed in her ears, and in the darkness under her blanket. She knew that night at the restaurant could not have been a dream. Those faces that had seemed to float in the nothingness outside the restaurant and the laughter that filled her ears now . . . in Mila's mind, they fit together like a cat and its meow.

Had it really been a week since they'd been at Etta's? Mila didn't remember anything happening since she ran out of the restaurant.

As sure as she was, though, her sureness began to fade when she thought about it. It was as if the memories of a week bubbled up and formed in her mind just when she needed them. After a moment, she became convinced that Mum was right. It had been a week. Images came to her, snippets of the last seven days, like the short clips before TV shows: *Previously in Mila's life. . .*

She lay there imagining it, with her voice narrating the last-week's highlight reel. A lunch of rubbery hotdogs and soggy chips with Junie in the cafeteria. Band practice after school on Tuesday. A chemistry quiz Mila had aced. She zoned out as she remembered snippets of her week, until suddenly she realized the laughter was gone. The room was quiet.

Total, complete silence. Not a whisper. Not a drip of water from the bathroom next door. There was not even the sound of Dad whipping up omelette after omelette, his whisk scraping against the metal bowl, which Mila woke up to nearly every morning. There was nothing.

Before Mila decided to stick her head out from under the duvet to check her surroundings, she already knew what she'd find. Darkness. An empty house. She'd find terrifying silence and pitch black. And if she looked up – particularly if she tried to run out of the house – she'd find the huge, hazy faces looking down at her. As they'd hovered in the nothingness outside Etta's Pizza Palace last night, the faces had made Mila's skin prickle with fear.

Or was it last week? Mila's head spun with confusion.

"I'm not doing this again," Mila said as she poked her head out and then rose from her bed. This time she didn't move cautiously. She didn't move with timidity. Whatever was going on, there had to be an explanation, and Mila was going to find it.

She grabbed her dressing gown from the back of her desk chair and stomped out of the room, into the dark upstairs hallway. In the bathroom, she flicked the light switch out of habit. Nothing happened, but she wasn't surprised. The shower, though – Mila hadn't expected that not to work. The knobs squeaked, but no pipes strained and no water sprayed out of the showerhead.

Mila thought she would try to wash her face in the sink, but even that was dry. She stomped her foot, left her dressing gown in a heap on the floor and went back into the dark hallway.

But as she stepped through the doorway, lights flashed, and she glimpsed a scene she wasn't expecting. Mila had been certain she'd just walked through the door from the bathroom to the upstairs hallway. But when she blinked, she opened her eyes to the kitchen. The door swung closed and open and closed and open behind her. Dad stood at the kitchen table, serving her a mushroom omelette and veggie sausages.

"Good morning, Sunshine!" Dad said. He dropped the plate of food at Mila's spot at the table.

Mila hopped onto her chair and leaned her chin on her folded arms, like it was the most ordinary morning ever.

"Slow to get moving this morning?" Dad asked. He pouted at her, and someone snickered.

"What was that?" Mila said. When she heard more laughter – as if in reaction to her confusion – she spun, desperate to find the source of the sound.

Mila jumped down from her seat and hurried to the swinging door, unsure what she would find on the other side. When she pushed the door open, she was surprised to find the living room.

Now Mila was worried. *Why is the layout of my own house confusing me so much?* she wondered. She could have sworn that when she had walked through this doorway before, she had come from the upstairs hallway.

Mila shook her head to clear away the confusion. The living room was lit and looking quite normal, but empty of people. There were no people gathered on the sofa, red-faced and grinning after a good guffaw – despite the sounds Mila had heard just moments ago.

"What was what?" Dad said.

Mila turned and watched him spear a sausage from his plate with a fork and pop the whole thing in his mouth. Dad's grin grew as he chewed. It made him look like a child for a moment, and the laughter swelled and faded again.

"Are Grandma and Grandad still here?" Mila asked.

Dad narrowed his eyes at Mila as if she was mad. He shook his head, his mouth too full to speak. Still, he tried: "Dey weft fwee days ago." Tiny bits of sausage fell from his lips, and the laughter exploded.

"Where is that laughter coming from?" Mila snarled, crossing the kitchen in three long strides to peer out of the back door.

"Laughter," Dad whispered. "Hmm."

Dad moved slowly towards the swinging door, keeping his suspicious eyes on Mila, and pushed the door open a bit. "Honey!" he called through the open door. "Call your cousin, the psychiatrist. I think Mila's cracking up!"

But the only cracking up Mila was familiar with was the laughter that seemed to roar in her ears now. It was as if the world were truly a stage, and her life was a sick comedy that everyone but her found hilarious.

"Ugh!" she grumbled.

She stomped past her father, but he grabbed her elbow and said close to her ear, "Nice improv, huh? They loved it."

Mila stumbled away as he let go of her arm. She backed through the swinging door to the living room, but she didn't end up in the living room.

She shouldn't have been surprised.

She should have known by now that the doors in her life couldn't be trusted. The fact that the kitchen door led her somewhere other than the living room shouldn't have been startling.

Mila found herself face to face with Junie Weid, not in her own living room – which would have been strange enough – but in Mr Hartly's maths class.

Mila gasped and grabbed at her shirt, panicked that her recurring dream of turning up at school in her pajamas had finally come true. She expected to look down at a knee-length T-shirt featuring a smiley-faced strawberry, but instead she found her navy blue school jumper, skirt and grey tights. When had she gotten dressed? And Mila's bag was at her feet. *Probably with that script in it,* she thought. When had she grabbed her bag?

"Mila," Junie said in an angry tone.

Mila looked up.

Junie gave her a withering glare, and her lips curved into a minor snarl. "Mila Chun," she said. "Are you even listening to me?"

"What?" Mila said. Somehow she was sitting at her desk. She couldn't be sitting. She was sure she hadn't sat down. She'd been walking – she'd been on her feet and *storming* into the living room, furious with

. . . with someone. Mila couldn't quite remember.

She'd been dropped into a scene and she'd missed the whole beginning. How long had Junie been talking? What had she been saying? Mila had no idea.

Mila squeezed her eyes shut and tried to remember. The memories popped into her brain just like they had in bed: showering, dressing, walking to school with Junie.

But the strain on her brain was too much. Mila's whole body went cold. Her eyesight began to darken at the edges, and her head went light.

She was suddenly very glad to be sitting, because if she'd been standing she would've certainly fallen over.

"Oh my gosh, Mila," Junie said loudly, getting up from her seat and crouching in front of her friend. Any irritation or wickedness in Junie's face fell away, suddenly replaced with concern. This was a rarity for Junie. "Are you all right?"

Every set of eyes in the classroom turned to watch Mila.

She shook her head at Junie, because she wasn't all right, but that just made her feel worse. "I don't know," she said, "I –"

She glanced towards the front of the room. Mr Hartly had stopped scribbling on the white board with his marker. He was halfway through some formula about functions and sine and cosine, and had stopped to stare at her. It made Mila's head spin even worse.

Ricky Chestnut was half turned around in his chair, also watching her. His rich brown eyes shined, and his eyebrows were raised in concern.

"Honey," Junie whispered as she followed Mila's gaze. "Oh no. Tell me you didn't do something absolutely moronic. Is that why you're feeling so icky?"

"What?" Mila said, baffled. "No, I didn't do anything. I'm just–" But she cut herself off. How could she possibly explain what she was experiencing?

Junie clucked her tongue and shook her head, disappointed. "You tried to talk to Ricky again, didn't you? I told you not to try that again without me around." Junie leaned in closer and whispered even more quietly, "Or without your script, for that matter."

Laughter exploded in the room, but Mila couldn't find a single smile on the faces of her classmates. In fact, aside from Ricky's glances in their direction, everything had returned to normal. Mr Hartly had even gone back to writing that bewildering equation on the white board.

But *someone* was laughing. In fact, judging by the sounds Mila heard, a hundred people were laughing, just like what had happened this morning in her kitchen.

"What *is* that?" Mila said, her voice too loud now. "Who is laughing?"

Mr Hartly turned away from the board and looked at Mila. Ricky Chestnut quickly looked away while the rest of the class turned in their seats to stare.

"Is something wrong, girls?" Mr Hartly asked.

"Um," Junie said, smiling and standing up. "Nothing serious. Mila's *definitely* not feeling well." She grabbed Mila's wrist and pulled her friend to her feet. "I'll take her to the nurse. Lady problems, you know." More laughter came, and seemed to flood the room.

Mr Hartly coughed into his fist and his face went red. "Yes, of course. Thank you, Junie," he said, setting his eyes on his pad of hall passes. He grabbed the pad and scribbled on it, then ripped off the top slip of paper for the girls. "Make sure she gets to the nurse okay. And please hurry back, Ms Weid."

Junie flashed a smile, grabbed the pass and tugged Mila by the elbow, snarling in her ear, "Come *on.*"

CHAPTER 6

The hall lights flickered the way they always did. Today, though, they flickered around in Mila's eyes and brain like a super-speed table tennis tournament. It made her head pound and her stomach twist. She groaned.

"Don't think for a minute I don't know what you've been up to, Mila," Junie said, not an ounce of sympathy in her tone. She dragged Mila down the hallway towards the nurse's office.

"No," Mila said. She tried to pull her wrist free, but Junie's grip was too strong.

"It's nothing like that. I didn't talk to him. I haven't even seen Ricky in a week. I think."

Junie rolled her eyes and spun to face Mila as they reached the door to the nurse's office. "Obviously I know that," she snapped. "You haven't even cracked the binding on the script, have you?"

"The script?" Mila said. Her head whirled now, and she had to clench her stomach tight to stop the queasiness. "The one – the one you wrote?"

"Are there other scripts in your life?" Junie said, her face centimetres from Mila. "Yes, the one I made. Have you read any of it?"

"I . . . I glanced at it," Mila admitted. "Just for some ideas to talk to Ricky. But it didn't go very well."

Junie put her hands on Mila's shoulders. "Read it, Mila," she said. For a brief moment, she seemed to really, truly care. "It will help."

Just then, the nurse's office door swung open and Mrs Barabasha stuck her head out, her reading glasses balanced on the tip of her nose. "Ladies?" she said.

Laughter. Applause. Cheering.

Mila thought she might fall over. She put one hand on the cold brick wall, hoping to steady herself.

Junie stood up straight and faced the nurse. "Mila is really ill," she said. "I turned to her in maths class and her face was pale and sweaty."

"Sweaty?" Mila mouthed at her, patting her forehead.

"I was sure she was going to faint at any moment," Junie said. "Of course I insisted to Mr Hartly that I be allowed to escort her to your office, as she is my dearest friend."

Mrs Barabasha smiled. She took Mila by the hand. "Thank you, Junie," she said. "You can go back to Mr Hartly's class now.

I'll see to your dearest friend's safety from here."

Mila waved limply to Junie as she retreated. Then she let Mrs Barabasha lead her into the office.

A round of applause swelled up as the door closed behind them, full of cheers and hoots and hollers. Whoever was clapping sure seemed to like Junie.

"Now, Mila," Mrs Barabasha said as Mila sat on the edge of the brown faux-leather examination table. "What's happening with you today, dear?"

Mrs Barabasha walked around her desk and sat in her chair.

"Another case of math-itis?" Mrs Barabasha said, laughing a little and bouncing her eyebrows.

Laughter.

"Because I've already had two of those this week," the nurse went on as she clicked around on her computer. "At this rate we'll have an epidemic."

More laughter.

It echoed in Mila's head. "Why won't it stop?" Mila muttered. She put her head in her hands.

"Lie down, dear," Mrs Barabasha said as she rose from her seat. Her desk was cluttered with figurines, including a flower that danced to the music coming out of a little portable CD player. It sounded like the lift-music version of a hit song, but Mila couldn't quite identify it. It sounded familiar, though, as if she had heard it a million times.

"When you say it won't stop, what are you referring to?" the nurse asked as she slipped a thermometer under Mila's tongue.

Mila shook her head. "I don't want to tell you," she mumbled around the thermometer. "You'll think I'm nuts."

"Try me," said Mrs Barabasha. She sat on the metal stool next to the long examination table where Mila lay. She had such a kind face. It was just the sort of face you would want your school nurse to have: round and gentle. She had a small mouth and big eyes that peered out from behind black-framed glasses.

She looks the part, Mila thought. As if the headmaster had hired an actress who fit the look of a nice school nurse. As soon as she had the thought, Mila wondered why it had crossed her mind. She didn't have much time to think about it, however, because just then the thermometer in her mouth beeped.

Mrs Barabasha pulled it from Mila's lips and looked at it over her glasses. "No fever," she said with worry in her voice. "Want to tell me what's going on?"

Mila sighed. What did she have to lose? She pushed herself up on her elbows. "I've been hearing things."

The nurse's eyes went wide, and then quickly narrowed. "What kind of things?" she asked.

"Laughter, mostly," Mila said.

Mrs Barabasha sighed. "Have other kids been laughing at you? Teenagers can be so cruel."

"No, not like that," Mila said. She struggled for the words to explain. "I mean big-time laughter – like the kind you hear on TV shows. And sometimes I hear cheering, too. They cheered for *you*, in fact."

"They?"

Mila felt her face go red. "The voices. Whoever it is. I don't know. Like a television audience."

"You mean like a laugh track?" Mrs Barabasha said.

Mila nodded and lay back. "I told you," she said. "Nuts."

"Maybe, maybe not," the nurse said. She gave Mila a sympathetic smile, then turned around and opened a cabinet. She grabbed a compress and twisted it till it popped to make it cold. Then she laid the icy strip of cloth-covered goo on Mila's forehead. "For now, we'll write this off as stress. You're in Year 10, right?"

"Yes," Mila said.

The nurse nodded knowingly as she stood up. "GCSEs can be extremely stressful," she said. "You've got all those big exams coming up. I'm sure you're worrying about getting a boyfriend or a girlfriend. All your friends are moving in different directions. You're probably facing lots of pressure to try things you're not sure you're ready to try. It can be very disorientating – very frightening even. How have you been sleeping?"

Mila couldn't remember the last time she'd actually slept. She strained her mind, trying to remember the last week. She tried to recall a single time she had actually brushed her teeth, put on her pajamas and gotten into bed. All she had were images – like the highlights of last week again. "I don't know. Not great, I guess."

"Then it's nap time," Mrs Barabasha said. "I'll turn the lights off, and you take the rest of the day to catch up on your sleep a little. Don't worry about your afternoon classes. I'll let the office know, and they'll notify your teachers. And if you need me, I'll be right here at my desk playing computer mahjong."

Laughter.

"Thanks," Mila said, and then she remembered coming out from under the covers that morning, and getting lost at Etta's Pizza Palace and being alone in the dark at home. She added in a panic, "But, um, leave the lights *on*, okay?"

Even in the tiny nurse's office – hardly big

enough to hold Mila and Mrs Barabasha – Mila heard dozens of people laughing. This time, though, she hardly noticed it.

Too tired to think, too tired to acknowledge the panic rising in her chest at the very sound of laughter, she closed her eyes. She could still sense the overhead light of the nurse's office behind her eyelids, but it actually helped her feel a little safer and a little more relaxed. Eventually, Mila fell asleep.

* * *

Mila woke in darkness. She lay on the examination table and stared up at the tiles of the ceiling. She listened but heard nothing. Maybe she had slept too long.

Maybe the day had ended, and Mrs Barabasha had gone home, forgetting about the student sleeping in her office. She would have turned the light off after Mila fell asleep, after all. No matter what Mila said about leaving the lights on, everyone knows that people sleep better in the dark. It would have been the decent thing to do.

Maybe the last bell had rung, and all the students left, and the lights were off because even the teachers and caretakers had gone home.

She hoped it was true. But she suspected it was not. She suspected it was happening again – whatever *it* was.

Mila got up, threw open the nurse's office door and ran into the dark hallway like a girl possessed.

"Hello?" she shouted. Her voice echoed through the school, looping around the hallways and bouncing off the ceilings and lockers till she heard her own cry over and over again.

But Mila heard something else, too. She heard a squeak. At first she thought it was a mouse scurrying around in the vents somewhere. But no – as it squeaked some more, Mila realized it was a wheel.

At the far end of the long and wide front hallway, a shadow fell across the white tiled floor. Something was coming.

When it had happened before – when the darkness and silence and solitude had come – Mila had been alone. She had been desperate then for anyone to come and find her and pull her out of the darkness and back to her normal, well-lit life. But now, in the huge, empty school with no idea of where to go or how to get there, someone was coming, and it terrified her.

Mila pressed her body against the wall as if she might hide from whatever approached, but it was no use.

She tried the doorknob of the nurse's office, thinking she would go back in there to hide, but it had locked behind her. She hustled down the hallway to try some of the classroom doors, but they were also locked. There was nowhere to hide.

Mila could see the front entrance, just down the hallway, and she could tell it was dark out.

She ran for the entrance – six sets of double glass doors, all locked with heavy chains. There was no getting out that way. She crouched where she was with her back against the doors and watched as the shadow grew shorter and shorter, and the squeak grew louder and louder, as whoever it was got closer and closer.

CHAPTER 7

Mila closed her eyes and clenched her fists and thought over and over in her head, *It's a dream. It's a dream. It's just a dream.*

It had to be a dream. With all the weird stuff that had been happening, what other explanation could there be?

"What are you doing here?" someone shouted. "Those are locked. You can't get out that way!"

She opened her eyes. A man in a dark green uniform pushed a wheelie bin down the hallway towards her. The long, narrow handle of a broom stuck straight up out of the bin. "Everyone went home hours ago," he said. He pulled the cap off his head and wiped his brow with the forearm of his sleeve. "What are you still doing here?"

Mila stood up, and the mad beating of her heart slowed down.

It was the caretaker, cleaning up after hours. She *had* fallen asleep in the nurse's office. This wasn't another attack of her madness, nor a dream. It was just a case of an absentminded nurse.

"I'm sorry," she said, forcing a limp smile to her lips. "I fell asleep in the nurse's office and . . . how can I get out?"

"Back doors are unlocked," the caretaker said as he pushed his wheelie bin past the front doors, towards the science and maths wing. He shook his head as he passed and mumbled, "Where do they find these kids? Unprofessional, every one of them."

Mila ran through the empty school, and

while she'd been scared and angry only moments ago, now she was relieved, even gleeful. There was nothing scary going on here at all. Just a weird afternoon. She could be home in fifteen minutes if she walked fast. Maybe the whole episode – the missing time, the empty house and restaurant, the lights without power and the kitchens without heat – was just a long dream she'd had as she lay on the couch in the nurse's office.

Mila knew that it was dark out already. But through the back windows that flanked the doors to the sports field, it looked *too* dark.

"No," she said out loud. This darkness was the same darkness that had lurked outside the restaurant, the unnatural darkness. Mila slammed open the door into the darkness, and the howling wind greeted her.

From behind her, Mila heard the heavy clank of the door closing and locking. She spun and grabbed the metal handle and tugged on it to no avail. She pounded her fists on the door, hoping against hope that the caretaker might hear her and let her in.

"Please!" she screamed. "I don't know where to go!"

She imagined the caretaker with his cap in his hands just on the other side of the door, shaking his head and rolling his eyes, muttering, "So unprofessional."

She pounded again, screamed again. No one came, so Mila turned her back on the door. With her head down, she started across the school's sports field, though whatever was under her feet didn't feel like rich soil and soft, green grass. It felt like a hard tarmac floor.

At the top of the field, beyond where Mila knew the tennis courts must be – if she could only see them – should have been West Elm Close. Beyond that, there should have been the south side of her neighbourhood. But there were no street lamps, no landmarks at all. Only her instincts guided her as she pushed on, leaning into the wind.

Nothing broke the darkness around her except for a few bright white lights. They weren't big enough to be a car's headlights, and they weren't on the road anyway. Instead they swung across the sky like low-flying aeroplanes. They seemed close for a moment, and then miles away.

Mila's eyes stung and ran with tears, burning from the harsh wind. She covered her face with her arm and peeked above her elbow to see, but any sense of where she was headed had vanished.

A white light, the brightest one yet, swung around in front of her. Mila stopped and watched it speed towards her and then away from her again. She waved her arms above her head and called out to it. "Help me! Please!" In the wind, however, she couldn't even hear her own voice.

Just as the light seemed to come back towards Mila, looking like it was about to strike her, it switched off, leaving her lost in darkness once again.

Someone grabbed her wrist, and a voice barked at her ear. Mila could feel the heat of breath on her neck. *"What are you doing?"*

CHAPTER 8

Mila tugged, desperate to escape from the violent hand in the dark. "Let me go!" she shrieked.

"Oh, I'll let you go," the voice hissed. Despite the bellowing of the wind, Mila heard him loud and clear. "And you'll never work again. You're completely unprofessional – the worst I've ever had to work with!"

"I don't know what you're talking about," she screamed, still struggling to get away.

But the man pulled her against the wind, his strong hand around her wrist.

"Have you even read the script?" he snarled beside her. "Now get back to the set. And if your behaviour doesn't improve, you can believe we will be making some serious *changes* to this production. Is that clear?"

"What?" Mila said angrily, her face getting hot. "No, it's *not* clear. I–"

He gave her wrist another tug to quiet her. Then he let go of her wrist and gave her a shove on each shoulder to urge her forward, but she lost her footing.

Mila stumbled several steps and collided with a wall – or so she thought at first. But she groped around, found a doorknob, and without thinking, turned it. The door flew open into bright light, and Mila tumbled through and onto the floor of her living room. She groaned and got up on her hands and knees, twisting her neck to check behind her. The bathroom door stood open.

From above her, Mila heard concerned gasps and amused snickers. Standing over her in a half circle and staring down at her were three familiar faces: her mother, her father, and –

No. It couldn't be.

But it was.

Ricky Chestnut.

Laughter filled the room like a swarm of wasps. This time there was no doubt in Mila's mind. Whoever was laughing, was laughing at her.

"What's going on?" she said, still dazed from her fall and the mysterious run-in in the dark and wind. It took all her effort to form the words and use her body, as if she'd just woken up from a restless sleep full of bad dreams. Her head began to spin as she climbed to her feet.

Ricky grabbed her elbow and helped her to stand. "There you go," he said, and he smiled gently as he put an arm around her shoulder. "You all right?"

"I – I think so," Mila said. She leaned against him, worried she might fall. "It's been a weird couple of days."

"Have a seat on the sofa for a minute," Ricky said, and he led her there with an arm around her and his free hand on hers.

Mum and Dad winked at each other. "You two probably want a pop – or an orange squash!" Mum said, pulling Dad into the kitchen.

"I'll make some squash," Dad said, nodding. "And a soufflé! From scratch. Right now. Should take a *very* long time." He winked at Mila, and then they were gone. She hardly noticed the laughter this time, sprinkled with *ooh*s and *ahh*s.

Ricky sat beside Mila on the sofa and cleared his throat. "So," he said. "Your parents seem nice."

"What are you doing here?" Mila said before she could stop herself. But to be fair, it *was* very strange that Ricky Chestnut was in her house.

"You were with the nurse all day, weren't you?" Ricky said. "Mr Hartly asked me to bring your maths homework over." He reached over the arm of the sofa and lifted the strap of Mila's bag. "Also, you left this in class."

"Oh," Mila said. "Thank you. But why didn't he ask Junie? She lives so much closer."

"He was going to ask her, but the weirdest thing happened," Ricky said, running his hand through his hair. "She never came back to class."

Mila rolled her eyes at Junie's behaviour. "Typical," she said.

Laughter bubbled around her. Shaking her head, amused, Mila whispered to herself, "I'm almost used to it by now."

"Used to it?" Ricky said. He cocked his

head to one side and furrowed his brow. It made him look like a confused puppy. "Used to what? Junie's behaviour?"

"Oh, no," Mila said. "I mean, yeah. I'm used to that, obviously. I meant the laughter I've been hearing." She clapped her hands over her face, mortified. "I can't believe I just told you I've been hearing laughter in my head!"

"Ah," Ricky said, nodding and smiling. "The laughter."

Mila nearly jumped with joy and grabbed Ricky's hand before she knew what she was doing. "You hear it too?" she said. "Oh, thank goodness. I'm not crazy."

"Well," Ricky said, moving away from her on the sofa a little. "To be honest, no. I don't hear anything. But I think I'm supposed to go along with whatever you say so you don't get violent or something like that. I've been told delusions can make people very angry if they are confronted with reality."

Laughter.

Mila stood up with her fists clenched and stomped her feet.

"See?" Ricky said. "You're angry already."

Laughter.

"Argh!" she squealed. She snatched her bag off the floor and stormed into the kitchen.

"Angry!" Ricky called after her.

Laughter.

Mila stopped just inside the kitchen and let the door swing closed behind her as Mum and Dad halted their whispered conversation to look at her. They both had playful grins on their faces.

"Ricky thinks I'm a madwoman," Mila said, and she slumped onto the counter.

Laughter.

"Aww, honey," Mum said as she rose from

her stool and put an arm around Mila. "Why would he think that?"

"Because I *am* one!" Mila said, wriggling out of her mother's embrace.

"I guess we'll have to keep her in the attic!" Dad said.

Laughter.

But Mila didn't laugh. Her eyes welled up with tears, and before she knew what she was doing, it all tumbled out. The laughter, the darkness, the gaps in time – everything. She blabbed it all.

Mum patted her shoulder. "Oh, honey," Mum said. "That was just a dream. You told me about that weeks ago, don't you remember?"

Mila shook her head and moved away from Mum. "No, no," she said, frustrated. "I thought it was a dream. I *hoped* it was a dream. But it won't stop. It's happened so many times. You say that was weeks ago, but to me it just feels like a few hours. I can't remember anything that's happened since then. I don't even know what's real anymore . . . and it's scary."

Dad frowned at her. "Honey," he said. "You're just–"

"And *now*," Mila said, gesturing wildly towards the living room, "the best-looking boy in school – who I've had a crush on forever – is in our living room, probably on the phone to 999. I bet he's asking them to back the ambulance up to our front door to collect me!"

Laughter exploded from every direction. Mila put her head in her hands and groaned.

Mum put her arm around Mila's shoulder. "He *is* very good-looking," she said, ignoring everything Mila had told her about the weird stuff that was still going on. She seemed determined not to notice all the strange things that were happening. Or maybe she really didn't see or hear them. Mila didn't know which possibility was worse.

"And he's charming!" Dad said as he got up from his stool to put an arm around Mila as well. "We had such a nice chat with him before you, err, *fell* out of the bathroom." *Hysterical laughter.* "Did you know Ricky's going to the county cross-country meet next weekend?"

Mila shrugged off her parents' affections and headed for the back stairs. "I'm going to my room," she said. "I have a splitting headache and I want to lie down. Wake me after Year 11 ends."

She regretted the quip immediately as chuckles and guffaws rose up around her.

"Wait a minute," Mum called after her from the bottom of the stairs. "What are we supposed to do with Ricky?"

"I don't know, Mum," Mila shouted down, her voice thick with sarcasm. "Adopt him?"

The house practically exploded with laughter, and Mila went into her room and slammed the door, dropping her bag beside her bed. She dived under the covers and pulled a pillow over her head, desperate to block out the sounds of laughter and applause.

And then she remembered: Junie's script.

CHAPTER 9

Mila jumped up from the bed and dug around in her bag. Old homework, torn-up glossy magazines, stray papers, pens and pencils – it all went tumbling to the carpet. Mila didn't care. She knew the script was in there somewhere.

"Aha!" she said as she spotted its sky-blue cover and black-tape spine. She tugged it out of the mess. *"The Real Mila,"* she read aloud, and then she opened the booklet.

The lights around her went dim, but a single spotlight shined on the script as she flipped through the pages.

The first scene showed her and Ricky talking in front of the school, with a bunch of boys on the school cross-country team watching as they waited for Ricky to get on the bus.

The second scene was of her running home, hurrying past the older girls on the way, and joking to herself about the "bladder matter".

The third scene included her saying hello to Grandma and Grandad despite the urgency of the bladder matter.

And so on and so on – it was all there. All of it, that is, aside from Mila's weakening mental state.

"Then I was off script," she said to herself as she sat on the edge of her bed with the script on her lap. "Mum and Dad weren't kidding. But how did they know that I was off script? After all, didn't Junie make this up?"

She pulled her mobile phone out of her pocket and fired a text off to Junie: *What the heck did you do?!*

She stared at the phone, waiting for a reply, but none came.

Mila flipped to the back of the script – past the scene she made in maths class when she was about to faint, past her visit to Mrs Barabasha's office, past sitting on her living room sofa and talking with Ricky while her parents poked their heads in and out of the room.

The next scene: Junie Weid knocks on Mila's bedroom door.

Knock-knock.

Mila gasped, and the door swung open.

"Are you decent?" Junie asked as she stepped inside the room. She sat down right beside Mila on the edge of the bed. "There are a couple of scenes left."

"What is this?" Mila said as she stood up

and backed away from Junie. "Is this some kind of elaborate joke? Is everyone in on this but me?"

"A joke?" Junie said. "No, it's nothing like that. It's a script. It's a TV show, Mila. And you're the star. You're the centre of everything!"

"But," Mila said as her skin went cold and tingly, "how?"

Junie stood up and crossed the room towards Mila. Mila backed away further till the backs of her legs struck her desk.

"The truth is, I thought you'd like it," Junie said. "After all, you always have been the centre of it all, haven't you?"

"What?" Mila said. "Me? What do you mean?"

"You don't know?" Junie said. "When your sweet best friend April Oak moved out of the house next door, to a new city all the way across the country, with no friends and no idea of how to make any, did you check in with her and see how she was doing?"

"April?" Mila said. "But how do you–"

"Did you even send her a text, offer moral support while she was adjusting to an entirely new school? An entirely new life?" Junie pressed.

"I'm sure April made new friends," Mila said. "Didn't she?"

Junie sneered. "Why don't you turn to the next page?" she said.

Mila had almost forgotten the thick script she held in her clammy hands. She flipped to the very end of the script and read aloud: "Mila checks her texts. She has one new message. It's from . . ."

She looked into Junie's face and finished the line: "April Oak".

Junie sat on the bed again, crossed her legs and smiled a sinister smile.

Mila grabbed her mobile phone and checked her text messages. There was one, and it was from a phone number she had never seen before. She was sure that it had to be April. It said, *I hope you enjoyed the show, but we have decided you're cancelled. Bye forever, right?*

"I don't get it," Mila said, confused. "Why? How?"

Junie stood up and moved towards the door. "She needed you," Junie said, "and you weren't there for her. You were too self-centred. Well now you're the centre of everything."

She stepped into the hall, into the darkness, and turned to face Mila again. The shadows fell over her like a curtain.

"Please," Mila said as she tossed the script aside. "I promise I'll make it up to you – up to April. Can't you tell her I'm sorry? Can't I tell her I'm sorry?"

"It's far too late for that," Junie said from the darkness. "Years too late, in fact. Goodbye. Forever."

She closed the door, and Mila ran to throw it open again, but it wouldn't budge. It must have been locked or jammed or both. She threw herself onto the bed and sobbed.

CHAPTER 10

She might have slept a bit. It was so hard to tell as she lay there, her mind bouncing from anxiety to anxiety like a rubber ball in a house of mirrors.

After a while, when the light outside felt like early nighttime and the house seemed very quiet, Mila sat up and looked around. Everything seemed so normal.

But everything was anything but normal. It had been a crazy few days.

No. Wait, she thought. *Not days. Weeks. Mum said weeks. Junie had just been here and –*

Mila couldn't remember. She sighed. "Hopefully Ricky's gone by now," she said to herself. "That is, if Mum and Dad haven't given him Anthony's room."

Mila chuckled at her own joke, but – and this made her heart skip a beat – no one else laughed.

"Hmm," Mila murmured, deep in thought. She stood up and paced her bedroom floor. "Maybe I should move up to the attic like a proper crazy girl."

Again, no one laughed, and Mila went on, "Mum and Dad can take me out for special occasions and trips to the doctor."

Still, silence.

Mila's heart pounded hard and fast and her breath caught in her throat. Was it over? Had her mental breakdown come to an end?

She threw open her bedroom door and hurried down the dark upstairs hallway.

"Mum!" she shouted as she ran towards the main stairs. "Dad! I think I'm all better. I think everything's fine!"

But downstairs, the living room was dark too. The air was still and cool. No silvery moonlight shined in through the big front windows. No dogs barked down the street. No headlights slid across the far wall. No birds sang, and no streetlamps flickered under an overcast sky.

Mila turned her back on the front windows and gasped. A light shined under the kitchen door, and Mila smiled.

"Mum?" Mila called as she hurried into the kitchen. She expected to find her mum standing at the counter, her hands wrapped around a cup of herbal tea. She often had one just before bedtime. Maybe Dad would be at the little table by the patio door, his laptop open in front of him, catching up on news from the worlds of sport and finance.

But Mila found none of that. Instead she found a man – a familiar man – dressed in dark green from head to toe, pushing a broom. Mila screamed.

"Oh, you're still here?" he said.

Mila ran to the cutlery drawer, planning to grab a knife in self-defence. Then she would get to a phone and call the police – but the drawer wouldn't budge. She tried another, and another, and then tried a cabinet. Nothing budged, as if they had been sealed shut with super glue. Maybe they weren't even real.

She pressed her back against the fridge and faced the man. "What are you doing here?" she snapped. "Aren't you the caretaker from the high school?"

He shook his head, not even looking up from his tedious task. He just kept pushing the broom and said, "You might as well go home. Show's over. Not being renewed."

"What show?" Mila said, her heart pounding with fear and confusion. "Renewed? What are you talking about?"

The man opened the patio door and pushed out the dust. "You gave it your all, kid," he said, leaning on his broom handle and putting his hand on his hip. "I've seen it a million times. They're not picking it up for another series. Don't blame yourself."

He picked up the broom and tipped his green cap. "Good night, miss," he said as he stepped through the patio door into the darkness beyond. "And good luck. I'm sure you'll find something else soon."

He closed the door behind him, and Mila hurried after him. "Wait," she said, throwing the door open again, but instead of the quiet darkness of her back garden in the evening, she was greeted by howling winds and pitch black, dotted here and there by white lights that seemed to dive and zoom.

She stood there in the darkness on the wooden deck, shielding her eyes from the wind as her hair whipped across her face. The white lights began to fade, and then they disappeared entirely. Soon the wind slowed and almost stopped, till it was less like a stormy gust and more like the cooling draught from an air conditioner.

Then only one light remained: a red one, flickering nearby. Mila moved towards it.

Her eyes grew accustomed to the dark. A shape began to form in the blackness – something huge, with the red light near its centre. It was taller than a person and wider. Beyond that, she saw what might have been hundreds of small buildings in the far distance.

No, Mila realized as she got closer to them. *They're close*.

She reached out and touched the red light, and then the hulking mass around it, made of metal and plastic and glass. "It's a camera," Mila whispered. "A television camera."

Beyond it was not the skyline of some far-off city. They weren't buildings. They were a hundred plastic chairs. Rows set up for an audience that wasn't there.

"The laughter," Mila said as her skin went cold. She shivered. "This is where the laughter was coming from. But this isn't a show. It's –"

She turned around, expecting to find her house – two storeys, painted pale yellow with white trim and a red brick chimney up the west side. She would see her own room, the window on the right on the second floor, with a dozen decals of kites in every colour. She'd seen her house a hundred times, from the back and the front.

But her house was gone, nothing more than a set. There were two walls and floors and a set of stairs to nowhere. "A soundstage?" Mila said.

She stepped closer to the stage, slowly and carefully. "But it's *real*," she said, louder now, as if someone might hear her and decide to help.

"Dad cooks dinner in there," she said, pointing at the kitchen. "And Anthony taught me how to tie my shoes right there. And Mum practises her clarinet there. She has for years! It's always been real!"

Mila faced the empty stands, pleaded with them. The warped faces that had looked down at her from the darkness like a panel of judges were now gone. Now the chairs were empty.

"*I'm* real," she pleaded. "I was born, and I had friends and I went to school. And I struggled with maths, and I knocked Mum's clarinet off its stand when I was seven! And Anthony crashed the car that Bank Holiday when Mum and Dad were out of town, and–"

The empty seats were silent, and the camera didn't pan – didn't follow her as she moved closer.

"Please," she said, pressing her hands against her chest. "I don't know where to go. I'm not a TV character. I'm Mila Chun. I'm *real*."

Silence. She would have done anything for another burst of laughter, another chuckle, another snicker, a round of applause, even an *ooh* or *ahh*.

With her head down, Mila walked back to the stage and stepped into the living room, though it was missing two walls and a ceiling.

On the coffee table sat a blue-covered book with a black-tape binding. Mila ran her hand over the cover and remembered. She remembered Junie, and she remembered

April, and she was sorry. But it was years too late for that.

She lay down on the sofa and stared up at steel rafters and dangling microphones, cables and air ducts. She could feel the cool draught of air conditioning on her face. At least that was real.

"*I'm* real," she whispered to herself. "I'm Mila Chun."

But nobody was there to hear.

GLOSSARY

antagonist person who actively opposes someone

bewildering confusing

bladder organ where urine is stored before your body gets rid of it

epidemic infectious disease present in a large number of people at the same time

improv short for improvisation, a theatrical technique; scenes or lines made up on the spot, without a script

inappropriate unsuitable for the situation

inseparable unwilling to be separated

predictable expected; able to be predicted or declared in advance

queasiness feeling of being sick to your stomach

renew bring back again after a short break

salvage preserve something from potential loss

violent showing or caused by great physical force or a strong feeling or emotion

wispy fine, feathery, barely there

withering scornful; intended to make someone feel humiliated

woozy unsteady, dizzy or dazed

DISCUSSION QUESTIONS

1. Throughout the story, there are points where Junie seems like a good friend to Mila and there are points where she seems like an enemy. Talk about how your perception of Junie changes throughout the book using examples from the text.

2. How does Mila come to the conclusion that she's a character on a television show? Discuss the clues that led her to discover that her life was not what she thought it was.

3. Imagine that Junie doesn't give Mila a script early on in the book. Talk about how you might have read the story differently.

WRITING PROMPTS

1. Foreshadowing is a technique authors use to give clues about events that will happen later in the story. Write a short essay explaining how the author of *Fade to Black* uses foreshadowing to give clues about what is going on with Mila.

2. Junie hands Mila a script to help her talk to Ricky. Do you ever wish you had a script to help you get through a conversation? Write a script for a made-up conversation you'd dread having.

3. Mila experiences a lot of uncertainties. She loses track of time, she can't remember what she's done or where she's been and she keeps experiencing strange phenomena like flashing lights, mysterious laughter and faces that seem to loom above her. Write a poem about one or more of these experiences from Mila's perspective.

ABOUT THE AUTHOR

Eric Stevens lives in St. Paul, Minnesota, USA. He is studying to become a middle-school English teacher. Some of his favourite things include pizza, playing video games, watching cooking shows on TV, riding his bike and trying new restaurants. Some of his least favourite things include olives and shovelling snow.

ABOUT THE ILLUSTRATOR

Neil Evans lives on the south coast of the UK with his partner and their imaginary cat. Evans is a comic artist, illustrator and general all-round doodler of whatever nonsense pops into his head. He contributes regularly to the British underground comics scene, and he is currently writing and illustrating a number of graphic novels and picture book hybrids for older children.

PSYCHOLOGICAL THRILLERS

Within the horror genre, there are many different sub-genres. One of these sub-genres is the psychological thriller, which tends to focus more on the emotional or psychological state of the characters rather than the plot. In most psychological thrillers, the action is limited. The horror instead comes in the form of characters battling their own minds, like Mila Chun does throughout *Fade to Black*.

Mila's perception of reality begins to fall apart in chapter one, when her best friend Junie hands her a script. Gradually, strange things start happening to Mila. First it's the sounds – laughter that reminds Mila of laugh tracks on sitcom TV shows and hollers from what sounds like an audience. Soon after, Mila starts to lose track of time. She goes into the bathroom in broad afternoon daylight and comes out minutes later to total darkness.

Later, Mila begins to see faces looming at her from the sky, and lights flashing in the distance. Along with her perception of time, she also starts to lose track of her memories. She remembers snippets of events, like flashbacks on a television show – finishing a maths test, talking with Junie in the cafeteria, walking home from school. In one scene, Mila's mother tells her to "stick to the script." Pretty soon Mila isn't sure whether her life is – or has ever been – real.

Psychological thrillers often include complex, strained relationships, like the one between Mila and Junie. Stories in this sub-genre tend to build tension throughout, and they rarely reach a clear solution by the ending.

What makes these stories so terrifying is that so many people are able to relate to the situations and characters on an emotional level. We have all felt suspicion, paranoia, distrust and self-doubt – characteristics that are often explored in psychological thrillers – in our own lives. By exploring emotions that people often try not to acknowledge, psychological thrillers unsettle their audiences and question readers' senses of reality.

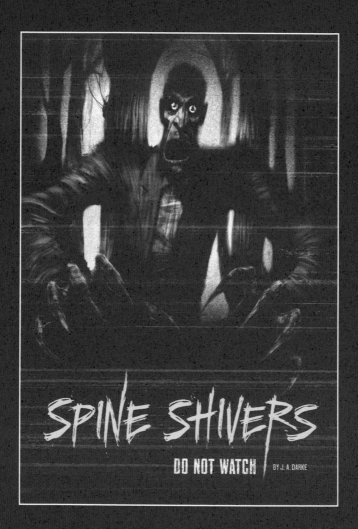

SPINE SHIVERS

DO NOT WATCH

BY J. A. DARKE

DO NOT WATCH

The Gaunt Man's face was ashen and empty of emotion. The hollows of his eyes were like inky pools of evil. He wore the same tattered black suit he'd been wearing in the film. His arms hung at his sides, too long for his body. The darkness of the room seemed to be drawn to him, wrapping itself around him.

Sam's heart thundered in his chest so hard he feared it would break his ribcage.

Hudson turned, and for the first time, he appeared to be terrified.

"Wha–" he stammered. "What is that?"

"It's the Gaunt Man," Sam whispered. "He's here for us."

The torch winked off for good.

The Gaunt Man did not move. He blocked the office's entrance – the only way out. Slowly, his arms rose. They reached out, stretching forward, hands and fingers like crumbling stone.

He was reaching for Hudson.

"No!" Hudson shouted. He stumbled backwards, tripping on a box and nearly falling. "Leave me alone!"

The Gaunt Man stepped forward. Shadowy tendrils snaked out of his suit coat and extended towards Hudson. As the Gaunt Man pursued Hudson, Sam saw his chance for safe passage out of the office. Hudson must have seen it, too.

"Sam!" Hudson shouted. "Sam! Get out of here!"

"No!" Sam shouted back.

"Don't be stupid!"

With one final look at Hudson, Sam found the strength to move again. He dashed towards the door, diary in hand. Black shadows clawed at him, trying to pull him back. But Sam was quick, and he raced out into the living room and headed towards the front door.

He fumbled with the deadbolt lock. With a thunk, it disengaged, and he swung the heavy wooden door wide.

Hudson's screams filled the house, the world, the universe. Sam wanted desperately to go back, but knew that he couldn't. It was too late. The only way to help Hudson was to find a way to kill the Gaunt Man.

Sam leapt off the front porch and ran into the night once again. It was more humid than he remembered, and a flash of lightning brought with it a rumble of thunder.

He made it to the fence, began to climb over and turned back to look at the house. The Gaunt Man stood in the doorway, watching him.

Hurry! Sam's voice screamed in his mind.

Sam pulled himself up onto the fence. The diary slipped out of his fingers and tumbled to the grass. "No!" he shouted. He considered leaping down to get it. But the Gaunt Man was gliding across the lawn now, heading for him.

I have to leave it.

Sam swung his legs over the metal fence and thrust himself forward. He fell headlong into the soil.

"Oof!" The air was driven from Sam's lungs. He gasped for breath and felt it burn in his chest. There was no time for pain, though. Sam rose to his feet, made sure his rucksack was strapped securely on his back and broke for the cornfield.

He ran in long strides, faster than he'd ever run before. Sam was not an athlete – in fact, he hated athletics more than any other sport – but he felt like he was racing in the Olympics. He pushed harder with each step, over clumps of soil and stone, putting as much ground as possible between himself and the Gaunt Man.

Cold raindrops fell suddenly from the sky like needles, striking his face and clothes. The soil around his feet was turning to mud. It felt like quicksand trying to pull him down. By the time Sam reached Hudson's car, he was drenched, his soaked clothes weighing him down. He fumbled for the driver's side door handle, praying that Hudson had left the keys in it.

It was locked. "NO!" Sam slammed a fist into the driver's side window. Then another. He wanted to break the window, to get in and get away. Rain coursed down the window and splattered with each blow.

Sam looked back. The Gaunt Man was nearing the edge of the field. He glided above the wet earth, and it appeared as if the falling raindrops were moving through him, leaving him dry.

Sam had no choice – he had to run. He ducked into the dark forest on the other side of the car.

It was cold and damp, but the canopy above kept most of the rain out. Tree branches clawed at him. They hooked his shirt and dug into his arms and scraped against his face. They did their best to trip him up. Sam staggered ahead, not sure where he was going or what he was doing. He could sense the creature at his back.

"Why?" Sam shouted. "Why are you doing this?" He felt hot tears burn the corners of his eyes. He stumbled, striking his shin against a log, and fell hard to the ground. Twigs snapped beneath him like tiny animal bones.

Sam panicked. He peeled off his rucksack, unzipped it, dug around and found the videotape. "Here!" he shouted, holding it out, searching the shadows for the Gaunt Man. "This is what you want! Take it!"

Nothing.

"I'm sorry," Sam said. "I'm sorry we watched it."

He flipped up the back of the video to expose the thick tape inside. Then, without thinking, Sam took the tape in his fingers and began to pull. The tape unwound like a spool of thread. It came out in long swatches, strands of it wrapping around Sam's fingers. The same wrenching sound of teeth on wood filled the forest and made Sam clap his hands over his ears.

The Gaunt Man stood before him.